ROSA JAMES

I0673296

THE BLOOMFIELDS

BY: ROSA JAMES

THE BLOOMFIELDS

Contact Information

Email: misuselsnake@gmail.com

Website: Passion2Right.com

@2024 Rosa James

Cover Art by Rosa James

Published by Passion2Right 07/30/2025

Edited by Chanekka Pullens

ISBN: 979-8-218-74480-9

1. *Fiction*

2. *Fantasy*

Printed in the USA

ROSA JAMES

TABLE OF CONTENTS

WARNING!!

This book contains profanity, sexual content and scenarios that could relate to true events.

 SPRING

Freya sat in the small, musty office watching the social worker make several phone calls to find her an emergency foster home. Just three hours ago, she was removed from the place she called home by CPS after her mother, Catherine, was found dead. The detectives were still at the scene investigating, unknowing that the thirteen-year-old possessed the answers they needed about what happened.

Days before Catherine's death, she returned home from a drug binge to rest. Freya hated it when her mother returned because she treated her badly. Freya was at her mother's beck and call, as if she was her personal servant. They never did anything fun together. Catherine never nurtured her daughter. Her addiction took presence over everything including Freya's wellbeing. When she had no money, Catherine prostituted her daughter so she could get drugs. How could a mother do such a thing! The final straw for Freya was when she ended up pregnant by one of the drug dealers. Instead of taking her to get an abortion at the clinic, Catherine beat her daughter and caused her to miscarry.

When her Uncle Kareem questioned what happened, Catherine lied. She convinced her brother that the beating was because she caught Freya skipping school at a boy's house.

Freya was angry with her uncle. Of all the lies Catherine told, and he chose this one to believe. With no one in her corner, the little girl would figure out how to stop becoming a victim of her mother's wrath. While recovering at home, Freya researched the best way to poison a person without leaving a trace. She was surprised to find out that the ingredients she needed were in her Uncle Kareem's garage. Freya mixed up a poisonous concoction and waited patiently. When Catherine demanded something to eat, Freya mixed the poisonous substance with the mayo and applied it to her mother's sandwich. After giving Catherine the sandwich, Freya hurried to her bedroom. That night, she tried to get some sleep, but the thought of her mother dying in the next room kept her up all night. The next morning, she entered her mother's bedroom to find her lifeless body. Freya took the sandwich and went to school with hopes her uncle would discover the body before she got home.

Before entering the school building, Freya discarded the sandwich inside the dumpster, then headed to class. Throughout that day, she looked at the classroom door patiently, waiting for someone to come inform her that her mother was dead. But no one came. When the dismissal bell rang, Freya dreaded going home. When she got off the bus, she walked down the block, observing her uncle's Buick in the driveway. The flat on the back passenger tire let Freya know that he had not been out. When she made it to the front door, she turned the key and entered. She found her uncle sitting in his normal place in the living room watching basketball and drinking beer. Instead of speaking, Freya went upstairs and peeked inside the bedroom. It sent chills through her spine seeing her dead mother still there.

Freya could not imagine sleeping another night with a dead body in the next room. She hurried downstairs to her uncle and expressed concern. Kareem ignored his niece because Catherine always slept for a couple of days after returning from a binge. Afraid to arouse his suspicion, Freya chose not to push the issue. Warily, she returned upstairs to her bedroom. Safe inside her room, she locked the door. How long would it be before her uncle noticed? That night, she lay in bed restless as she waited for her uncle to come upstairs. But the sound of loud music and scent of weed let her know he was not going to bed anytime soon. Freya allowed her thoughts to wander until her body was so tired she fell into a deep sleep.

In the middle of the night, Kareem stumbled down the long narrow hallway heading to his bedroom. When he saw Catherine's door open, he went inside to check. "Hey, sis, are you good?" he whispered, entering the room. As he eased closer to the bed, an eerie feeling came over him. It was too quiet and still inside the room, reminding him of when they found his grandmother dead. His feelings were validated as he looked down at his older sister's lifeless body. He kneeled and nudged her. "Catherine!" Her body was cold. He jumped back and stood there for several seconds. He questioned himself if this was real. Was the only person he considered family really gone? Despite Catherine's dysfunctional lifestyle, her presence would be missed. It was funny how a person could cause so many issues that you dread them, but once they die, you ache for them. Was it because at that point you only saw the good memories instead of dwelling on the bad ones? Snapping out of his thoughts, he hurried downstairs and called the paramedics.

A while later, Freya was awakened by all the commotion. She opened her bedroom door right in time to witness the Medical Examiner rolling her mother's body down the hall. She eased out the door and hurried downstairs, where Kareem was talking to the police.

"On the first and fifteenth of every month, Catherine leaves and goes on binges until her money is gone. Then, she comes back and sleeps for a couple of days." When he saw Freya, he gestured for her to come over before continuing, "This is her daughter Freya. Without her mother, I cannot continue to provide care for her." He placed his hands on her shoulders and kneeled to meet her eyes. "Freya, your mother is dead, and you will have to go into foster care."

Freya was livid! Why was her uncle giving her up to CPS! He was not the perfect parent, but he had always taken care of her, making sure she had all the necessities. Freya was sad and began to cry. It was terrifying not knowing where she would end up. She heard a lot of horror stories about foster care. There was even a group home a couple blocks away and the children there seemed worse off than she. She did not think this far into her plan, now her living situation could get worse. But despite the uncertainty of where she would go, she did not regret killing her mother.

Freya's thoughts were broken by the social worker speaking, "Thank the man upstairs because I finally found you a placement. It seems like the older a child is, the harder it is to find a good home." The social worker got up from her chair. She grabbed her purse and car keys before gesturing for Freya to follow. As they walked down the hall and got on the elevator, the only thing that Freya could think about was how dreadful the forest green sweater looked on the social worker. *Who would pick such a color to wear?* She thought.

The elevator ride from the third floor down to the garage seemed to take forever. Freya hated elevators and this old elevator seemed like it would malfunction at any time. The lights were dim, a few of the buttons were missing on the panel, the rug was dingy and worn, and the brown panel walls were depressing.

Reaching floor G, Freya followed the social worker off the elevator. As they walked, she noticed there were over a dozen identical cars with the "State of Missouri" license plates on each of them. They entered one of the cars and exited the parking lot.

As they rode, the social worker consoled her, "Don't worry, you are going to be okay. I found you a good placement, so you will not have to go to a group home. These people are new foster parents, so make a good impression." Freya nodded and continued to look out of the passenger window. Hungry, the social worker pulled into a fast-food restaurant parking lot. Freya's stomach growled when she smelled the aroma of food as the social worker parked. They exited the car, went inside, ordered dinner, and ate in silence. After finishing, they took a bathroom break before leaving. For the next half hour, Freya and the social worker rode silently until they arrived at the prestigious area on the outskirts of the inner city known as The Valley.

⊞NEW HOME

Arriving, the social worker turned onto a private road. Freya's eyes widened as she noticed the beautiful mansion they were heading towards. The journey to the mansion offered a beautiful early spring scenery. Freya admired the trees, various plants, and most of all, the lake.

"Wow! This is a really nice place," said the social worker, who was now parking the car in the circular driveway. She exited the car, went to the back-passenger door, and opened it, retrieving a black trash bag of clothing. Now outside the car, Freya walked toward the mansion slowly, admiring the stone exterior and large windows.

Before they made it to the door, it opened and a woman greeted them, "Welcome! I am Vita Bloomfield, but please, just call me Vita." She gestured to her son Viktor to come outside and grab the black trash bag from the social worker.

Once inside the foyer, both the social worker and Freya looked around in amazement. Everything was clean and decorated elegantly. "Let's go into the sitting area and get acquainted," instructed Vita, walking ahead. Freya gave her a once over. Vita was tall with a slim build. She strutted wearing a black leather pencil skirt, white blouse and black five-inch heels. Her skin made Freya think about milk chocolate. She wore her silky jet-black hair in a bob cut with perfectly trimmed bangs that complimented her high cheek bones and green eyes. Freya was intrigued by her beauty and assumed she worked in an office based on her attire.

"Vita, you have a lovely home. Do you have any other children here besides your son?" questioned the social worker.

Vita invited them to sit down before responding, "The young man that took the bag is my son Viktor. He comes home from boarding school during breaks and some weekends. I also have a daughter, Autumn, who is away at college. She will be coming home this weekend to meet Freya." While looking around, the social worker inquired, "Vita, will your husband be joining us this evening?"

Vita smiled. "Thomas is away on business. He will be home in a week." The social worker nodded and continued, "What made you two decide to become foster parents?"

"Well, I tried to have another child, but unfortunately, money can't pay for everything." Vita paused to offer Freya some tea and cookies from the table. "Once we decided to just adopt, my career took a turn, and we decided that a baby in the house would not work for our lifestyles. So, my husband and I decided to seek a child that was more independent." She took a cookie from the plate and bit it. The social worker admired the beautiful woman while wishing she had the energy to keep herself up so well.

"Wow! That's very interesting. We rarely find people that will take teens. Tell me, would you be interested in more children? The system is in desperate need of families for our older placements." Vita answered quickly, "Well, I am not trying to start a group home. Besides, this is our first go around. Let's see how this works out and we can revisit that conversation later."

Suddenly, they were interrupted by Viktor entering the room after taking Freya's belongings upstairs. "Freya, Viktor will give you a tour of the place and show you to your suite," said Vita.

Freya stood and said goodbye to the social worker before following Viktor out of the sitting room.

While Vita and the social worker went over everything, Viktor gave Freya a grand tour of the Marchbanks mansion. It had ten suites that were huge. They were all equipped with large walk-in closets and private bathrooms. Four of the suites were for guests while the other six were occupied by Vita and her children. The guest suites were painted and decorated with various neutral colors that reminded Freya of the fancy hotel rooms she saw on television. The other six suites were uniquely decorated. The first suite Viktor showed belonged to Vita and Thomas. Inside, Freya looked around, taking in the fresh linen scent. Everything was pure white with a red accent. Massive black and white photos of the couple in intimate positions, but not too explicit. Viktor explained, "My mother and stepfather can be very intimate at times." Freya focused on the massive canvas of Vita naked under a silky white sheet. In the photo she exposed just enough skin to make the photo provocative. Her hazel green eyes seemed to peer into Freya. She was so caught up in the photo that she did not hear Viktor speaking to her until he placed his hand on her shoulder. "Girl, that photo does the same thing to me. Let's get out of here."

The next suite belonged to Autumn. It had gold walls and an assortment of colors, from turquoise to hot pink. The design reminded Freya of an Arabian princess. The third suite consisted of purple and pink. Viktor did not disclose whose suite it was, but she could tell it belonged to a girl. The next suite was clearly a man's room. It was blue with camouflage décor. BB guns hung on the wall, along with a locked gun cabinet, and a shelf that displayed multiple trophies. Viktor spoke, "This is my stepbrother Jaquan's suite." He hurried Freya out and closed the door. The fifth suite was Viktor's. When Freya walked into his suite, the first thing she noticed was the fresh scent of lavender oil burning. The walls were painted beige and displayed big canvas photos of art. The cherry wood floor was complimented by big fluffy white rugs, and the furniture was white. Everything in the suite was so relaxing, crisp, and clean.

"I know what you are thinking! No, I will not trade with you. But your suite does have a wonderful view of the lake that I yearn for. Anyway! I love to see people's reactions when they enter. But don't worry, I have truly saved the best for last. And that is your suite!" Viktor clapped his hands as he hurried down the hall.

He opened the door and allowed Freya to enter first. The lights automatically came on, displaying the beautifully decorated space. Freya was overwhelmed with excitement. The bedroom at her uncle's house was a closet compared to what she was witnessing. Everything was perfect from the amber rose pink walls with many framed posters of teenage celebrities to the king-sized bed. There was a black couch that was decorated with zebra print and pink pillows and a zebra print furry area rug. Every electronic device, from a desktop computer, bluetooth speakers, a music keyboard, iPad, to a 50-inch television mounted to the wall.

The massive picture window displayed a view of the lake and there was a double door leading to a private balcony. When Freya entered the walk-in closet, it was empty. But she could imagine filling the closet with clothes, shoes, and accessories. Viktor read her mind. "Don't worry, we will have this closet filled in no time." He led Freya out of the closet and into her personal bathroom. Freya was astonished when she entered. There was a large tub, vanity, and another window that displayed a view of the lake.

Viktor said, "My sister decorated the suite months ago." He walked over to the bathroom window. "I so envy your view of the lake. Mother would never let us get this suite. She said it would be the perfect nursery when she had another baby."

When they exited the bathroom, Viktor plopped down onto the bed. "So, tell me where you are from. I am going to enjoy having a little sister. Autumn can be mean at times and my younger sister Jada is not around. I cannot wait to take you shopping! And by the way, that black trash bag is already in the trash where it belongs!"

Freya laughed. She took a seat on the couch before responding, "I am from inner Kansas City, Missouri. My mother and I lived with my uncle until she was found dead this morning." She attempted to appear sad. Viktor placed his hand on his chest. "Oh, no, I am so sorry about your mother! Was she sick?" Freya tossed around one of the zebra print pillows while answering, "You can say that. She was a drug addict. I think she took some bad drugs. If she were

18

truly sick, we would never know because she was not the type to go to the doctor for anything. It was like the drugs were more important than anything else."

Viktor's hand was still on his chest. Freya observed his freshly manicured nails as he spoke. "Wow, I know there is nothing that can bring her back. But look at the bright side of things, you are now out of that destitute environment. Your mother is no longer suffering and struggling with addiction. And to top things off, you now have a fabulous older brother. So come on, let me show you the rest of the place. Then, we will grab a snack and something that will relax you more." He got up and headed out of the suite.

Freya gave her new suite another look before catching up with Viktor halfway down the hall. When they returned downstairs, the social worker was gone, and Vita was nowhere in sight. Freya inquired, "Your mother said you go to boarding school. Isn't that some form of punishment?" Viktor strutted at a fast pace through the foyer, never looking back at her. "Yes, to them it is a punishment. But for me, I am living my best life there. To be surrounded by so many handsome men is a dream come true for me." Freya laughed at his statement. Viktor was young, entertaining, confident and had no shame in expressing his sexuality. His sexuality was the reason why Thomas talked Vita into sending him to boarding school. But Viktor was glad to be away from home and never resented his mother for agreeing. However, Vita carried the guilt every day. She should have loved her son and embraced him instead of allowing Thomas's point of views to control the situation.

The remainder of the tour included the library, Vita and Thomas's home office, the formal dining room, the indoor sunroom, the entertainment room, indoor basketball court, indoor pool, second family area, an indoor shooting range below the mansion, and the back patio. Viktor saved the kitchen for last because he was hungry. He went to the refrigerator to grab some snacks. Freya took a seat on one of the bar stools at the massive marble island. Viktor retrieved a Charcuterie Board and placed it on the island. "Oh, yeah, you'll be home schooled until you are in high school. Do you like cheese and wine?" Freya was taken aback by the wine question. "Um, your mother allows you to drink wine. Isn't that alcohol?"

"Yes, it is. But mother allows us to drink one glass of wine daily. And of course, I take advantage of that." He began laughing as he grabbed two wine glasses from the cabinet. Freya observed him filling the wine glasses halfway. He slid one over to her. "If you are a beginner, then just take a sip every seven minutes. It will balance you out, trust me," he advised.

For the next couple of hours, they sat in the kitchen, ate cheese and olives, sipped red wine, and talked. When the wine started taking full effect, Freya retreated to her suite. She soaked in the tub for a half hour before slipping into some nightclothes that Viktor left on her bed. As she laid comfortably, she stared at the ceiling thinking about her day before drifting away into a deep sleep. But at 3:00am, she was awakened by someone in bed with her. When she opened her eyes, Viktor was sleeping next to her. The nightlight was dim, but she could see that he had a fresh bruise on his face. Suddenly, she noticed a person standing in the doorway. She was for sure the manly silhouette was not Vita, so she acted as if she was asleep. Finally, after a few minutes, the person closed the door. She heard footsteps heading down the hall, followed by a door slam. Now restless, she grabbed her iPad from the nightstand and began scrolling the internet. She made a mental note to question

Viktor about what happened to his face and who was the mysterious person lurking around the mansion in the middle of the night.

⚠ NOT SO PERFECT

Despite the wine and interruption of sleep, Freya awakened before Viktor, who was snoring. She got out of the bed and looked out of the window, admiring the view.

A few minutes later, Viktor awakened. "See, I told you the view was amazing. We should hang out on the dock when it warms up," he spoke, easing himself into an upright position on the bed. Ignoring his statement, Freya questioned, "What happened to you?"

Viktor grimaced while easing out the bed. "Let's just say Jaquan and I have not been getting along for the past few months." Freya headed to the bathroom. "I wonder if that was him standing in the doorway last night." She turned on the water in the tub for Viktor to soak.

Viktor winced as he entered the bathroom and spoke in a low voice, "Yeah, it was him. I am sorry if I surprised you when you woke up to find me in your bed asleep. But I knew he would not come into your room, so it was a safe place for me. When Autumn is home, I would go to her suite. Like I mentioned before this has been going on for the past few

23

months. He thinks I have something to do with our younger sister, Jada, disappearing last Christmas. Seriously, I think she is dead but mother said she ran away from home because she found the letter." He undressed, not caring about Freya being in the bathroom. As he submerged himself in the steaming water, Freya searched the cabinet and found some Epsom salt. Viktor watched her pour a generous amount of Epsom salt into the water. "I remember Jada used to look after me like this. You remind me so much of her. In fact, you two could pass for sisters." He closed his eyes and continued, "But no worries. We are going shopping today and we will discuss everything you need to know." He submerged himself further down in the tub.

"So, the purple suite belongs to Jada?" questioned Freya, now sitting on a bench in the bathroom. Viktor kept his eyes closed and nodded. There was silence for several seconds before Freya stood from the bench and exited the bathroom, leaving him to soak. A half hour later, she went back to check on him. Viktor was no longer in the tub and the bathroom was empty. She cleaned out the tub and did some hygiene. She exited the bathroom with plans to wear the same clothing since Viktor had thrown her belongings away.

However, when she exited the bathroom, she found a brand-new outfit laid out from shirt to shoes.

She dressed quickly and admired herself in the full body mirror. Everything fit just right. Viktor returned to the suite without bothering to knock. He playfully nudged Freya out the way and admired his attire in the mirror. His black eye was not stopping him from dressing in sea pink from head to toe. Freya was digging his prep boy look. "Girl, I love me some Tommy Hilfiger," said Viktor, strutting out the suite. Freya followed. They headed downstairs and found Vita in the office handling important paperwork. After examining Viktor's face, Vita gave Freya a black credit card and warned her that she would not refill it until next month. She returned to her paperwork. As they exited the office, Viktor whispered, "Don't worry, it's more than enough on there, she just likes to threaten us as if the money is going to run out." Freya laughed as she followed him out of the double door entryway, outside to a black Range Rover that was parked in one of the parking spots.

Freya took account of the brand-new black on black Cadillac and Lexus sedans as well as the white Jeep Rubicon. Everything was like a dream for her. Killing her mother had blessed her with a new family and she looked forward to living the lavish life they offered. While Viktor drove down the long driveway onto the road, Freya looked out the window admiring the beautiful natural scenery. Her life of misery was now a fairytale, but deep down she could not help but think about Jada.

Once they were a mile away from the estate, Viktor spoke, "Okay, young lady, if you don't know by now, you will learn later that I am the best child Vita has!" He laughed. "Now, I attend boarding school, but I will be home for the summer since you are here. Autumn will be home in a few hours, so you will get to meet her in the flesh." He stopped at the red light. Freya observed his demeanor change. He seemed to sit in a daze. When the light turned green, seconds passed before the car behind them honked, breaking his trance. He glanced into his rearview mirror briefly while driving. He hated talking about his younger sister, but since Freya was living with them, she had to know what happened.

"Jada is fourteen years old. The fact that my mother does not discuss it makes me think she is covering something up. I know for a fact that Jada would not run away because she was spoiled rotten. Now don't get me wrong, I am glad that you are here, but I find it ironic that you arrived right before Jada's birthday. Then Jaquan has been searching the property convinced that Jada is somewhere dead and buried." Now Freya's fairytale was turning into a law-and-order episode as she continued to listen. But a missing girl would not change her mind about living on the Marchbanks Estate.

Viktor continued, "So, just to break down our family history. My mother's father Octavious Marchbanks was wealthy. He was born in a shack in Tulsa, Oklahoma and lived in poverty for most of his childhood. At age eleven, my grandfather found his father hanging from a tree, so his mother packed up and headed north. They were homeless and my great grandmother was forced to prostitute for money. Then she met this wealthy man who became a consistent client. Eventually he fell for her, and they married. He took them away and that is when the good life started. The man taught my grandfather everything about making money and he listened. By the time my mother was born he was one of the wealthiest black men in the city. He had many investments in major businesses all over the world; so, my mother had money and inherited the Marchbanks Estate.

Then, she married my father, Samuel Covington, who was also well off. My father was a silver spoon kid but had to face the challenges of being a black boy in a white community. His parents were what I called the house niggas. They kept their heads down and were flexible to keep what they had worked so hard for. But that all changed when the community tried to bring my father down by accusing him of raping a white girl. That almost sabotaged he and my mother's relationship, but they got through it. When they decided to make it official, my mother convinced him to move onto the Marchbanks Estate because she did not want to leave or sale it. My father agreed and they grew their family. Autunm was born, then me, and we were one big happy family.

My mother got pregnant with Jada. Before she gave birth my father died of a heart attack while driving. I was three years old. After his death, my mother stayed home and took care of us. Then, Thomas came into the picture with his son, Jaquan, and moved in not even a year after my father's death. My mother continued to stay at home until Jada was twelve years old, before she pursued her dream of working in politics. And now, she works with the mayor. She doesn't need the money; she just loves politics and need something to do with her time."

He took a drink of his bottled water. "Thomas travels around the world securing business deals for a company known as Bloomfield Inc. As for Jaquan, he graduated from military school and was preparing to enlist in the navy when Jada disappeared. Every chance he gets, he takes his frustration out on me. I tell you; he has serious anger issues. Honestly, I really think he is homophobic." Freya could not do anything but say, "Damn." She was loving her new life, but it seemed to come with a lot of drama. However, it was not worse than the life she came from and what she did to her own mother; so, she would not judge and stick around. The Bloomfield family secrets seemed more interesting than the lavish life. Freya wanted to learn more about the family. She would continue to observe and be prepared for anything.

When Viktor parked at the outdoor shopping center, Freya was overwhelmed as she looked around at all the different stores that she had only seen on television commercials. They got out and started walking in the direction of the stores. Viktor turned, aiming his key fob at the jeep to make sure it was locked. "So, do you have a style in mind?" Before Freya could answer, they were disturbed by a female voice, "She's a vintage type of girl like me." Viktor turned quickly. When he saw his older sister, he ran over. Freya watched as Viktor hugged and planted kisses on her face. Autumn softly pushed him away. "Don't kiss me with those lips! When was the last time it has been wrapped around a hard one?" She laughed, walked over to Freya, and gave her a warm embrace. "Wow! She looks just like Jada." She then focused on Freya's hair. She frowned, trying to work her fingers through the kinks. "Okay, first off, we need to hit up the salon to get something done to this hair. Trust me, you will feel better shopping after your glam up."

Freya nodded in agreement as she admired Autumn's features. She had long jet-black hair that she wore straight, her skin was dark brown and smooth like silk, she had her mother's green eyes, slim build, and was dressed sophisticated. Autumn led the way. "Follow me. I know a great place to get your hair done." Viktor rolled his eyes as he followed the two girls. He was glad to see his sister but hated when she took over things. When Jada was around, she looked up to him and Autumn despised that. Viktor knew that Autumn was going to try and get Freya into her pocket.

But if Freya were anything like Jada, she would see Autumn for who she was. But little did Viktor know; Autumn was on a whole other level and gaining Freya's attention was far from the goal.

When they entered the salon, the receptionist greeted both Viktor and Autumn by name. "Does anyone have an opening for this lovely lady? She needs the full package," said Viktor, taking a seat in the empty barber chair. One of the stylists came from the back of the salon and instructed Freya to follow her to the shampoo bowl. "Freya, we will be back in an hour or so. Then, we can go shopping!" yelled Autumn from the front of the salon.

"Don't worry, she is in good hands," responded the stylist, checking the temperature of the water in the shampoo bowl. Autumn and Viktor exited the salon and headed to a nearby coffee shop to wait for Freya and catch up. Autumn purchased two mocha lattes. She returned to the table and took a seat. "I see Jaquan banged you up again!" Viktor grabbed his latte and took a sip. "I just don't understand why he hates me or even feels that I have something to do with Jada's disappearance. I miss her and want to know where she is too! It's like mother is just accepting the situation and no longer fighting for answers. I just don't understand why she is not using her people in high places to find my sister." Autumn gazed out the window, she knew her brother was right. Why was her mother not doing anything? It seemed like she had accepted things and was moving on. Autumn was fine with that but did not want Viktor to know how she really felt. In her eyes, Jada was an opinionated spoiled brat.

"You know mom is all about the image. She is off into politics and the last thing she wants anyone to know is that the perfect Bloomfields are dealing with a tragedy," said Autumn. She looked around. "So, does Thomas know about Freya yet? I am sure he has not come home in weeks." Viktor answered, "I am not sure, but I overheard mother saying that she and Thomas wanted an older child instead of a baby." Autumn laughed, almost spitting her latte out. "Mom with a baby? Could you imagine that!" They both shared laughter as Autumn continued, "To be honest, I think Freya is the perfect distraction because I don't think Jada is coming back."

Viktor leaned in and spoke in a low voice, "Sis, coming back? I think our sister is dead. It does not make sense for her to run away. You know I learned that our late father had a lot of enemies and unsettled debts linked to the mob. What if someone saw an opportunity and took it out on Jada? Everyone thought that Jada was his daughter."

Autumn nodded in agreement. "I could see that being a possibility. But remember, I found the letter she wrote. She was unhappy for some reason. Viktor, this money shit is not all it's cracked up to be. Rich people are just as miserable as poor folk." Viktor disagreed. "Shit! I love my fabulous rich life!" His elevated tone attracted some of the people in the coffee shops' attention. They spent the next couple of hours catching up before returning to the salon where the stylist was just finishing Freya's hair. Viktor walked up the middle of the booths vogueing. "Slay, baby, slay!" Some of the customers giggled while others snared. Autumn nodded in approval. "You look beautiful. Just put the charges on my mother's bill." She gestured for Freya to come to her. Viktor and Freya followed Autumn out the salon.

For the next few hours, the three shopped at various stores, loading both Autumn and Viktor's cars with clothing, shoes, and accessories. Afterwards, Autumn surprised everyone with dinner at her favorite sushi bar. They went inside. Autumn confirmed the reservation, and they all followed the host to their table. "Have you ever had sushi?"

"No, but I like to try new things," responded Freya, taking her seat. "Well, then you are my type of girl!" Autumn giggled, also taking a seat. After the waiter took their drink order, they continued conversating.

"Freya, I heard about your mother's death, I am so sorry. Tell me, how you are holding up?" questioned Autumn. Freya forced a sad face. "I really miss her. I don't understand why God took her away from me." Freya managed to get a couple of tears to stream down her face. Autumn reached over the table, placing her hand on top of hers. "Oh, sweety, I am so sorry to upset you." Viktor intervened, "I know it takes time to get through the pain. But trust we have your back and will love you like real family." Their moment was disturbed by the waiter placing their drinks on the table, proceeding to take their orders.

After receiving their food, the three enjoyed dinner while talking. During the conversations, Freya had to keep reminding herself that this was all real. She went from living a traumatizing life with her mother and uncle, to now living the finest life. Just thinking about all the items she had in the car she purchased gave her a surge of happiness. Both Autumn and Viktor were so nice and welcoming. She knew they would be great older siblings.

When finished, they headed home. When everyone arrived, Vita was waiting for them in the family room, enjoying wine and a book by her favorite author Rosa James. When Autumn entered, Vita got up from the couch and hurried over to her daughter, greeting her with a warm hug and kiss. While they greeted each other, Freya and Viktor put their bags away. When they returned, Vita and Autumn were catching up.

Freya took a seat on one of the plush cream sofas and watched them. Vita was very attentive and loving to both Viktor and Autumn. In Freya's eyes, she could not see Vita harming her children or even being okay knowing that someone else was. Now her question was, if Jada ran away from home, what would make her want to leave such a rich and loving life? She made a note to bring Jada up to Vita when the opportunity presented itself. She was good at reading people's energy and all she needed was to observe Vita's reaction at the sound of Jada's name.

A little after midnight, everyone retreated to their suites. Freya hung her new clothes and placed her new shoes on the shelves inside the walk-in closet. When finished, she stood back, observing the now half full closet. All her wants and needs were taken care of. She no longer had to worry about food, wearing worn dingy clothing, her mother coming home to mistreat her, being violated by random men, or dealing with her uncle's drinking and carelessness. Without those worries she had room to focus on the things that made her happy. Like filling the other half of her closet, sitting on the lake enjoying the scenery, relaxing, and watching her favorite television shows. She could focus on writing poems and make new friends. The possibilities now seemed endless. This was an example of how living felt verses just surviving.

Next, she showered before laying in her bed. As she watched the large black ceiling fan circulate slowly, the invasive thought of Jaquan standing at her door made her paranoid. She jumped from her bed and made sure the door was locked. Feeling secure, she returned to her bed and fell into a deep sleep.

SUMMER

Freya sat admiring the view of the lake from her window. Months had passed since she moved in with the Bloomfield's. Although she was concerned about Jada's disappearance, she would not trade living with the family for the world. Her final assignments for home school were completed and she was ready to enjoy the summer. She walked out onto her private balcony, taking in the warm June air. She could not wait until Autumn and Viktor returned from their schools for the summer so they could spend time together.

The upside of both Autumn and Viktor being away was that she and Vita were spending a lot of time together. Jaquan continued to search the woods for Jada, only coming inside to eat and shower from time to time. Thomas came home to meet Freya, but he spent more time away on business. It made her question whether he was on board with being a foster parent because he was never around. However, despite Freya's concerns, she and Vita were establishing a bond that could not be broken. The love and nurturing she was receiving from Vita seemed to make up for all the years she had endured abuse from Catherine. Freya took a seat on the chair and talked to herself, "Wow, I still cannot believe I am living here."

Suddenly, Vita disturbed her. She was standing in the doorway with a comb and a bottle of leave-in conditioner. She walked over to Freya and began parting her hair into sections so she could detangle it. "It's so beautiful out here in the summer." She applied leave-in conditioner to her hair as she stated, "Everyone will be home in a week." The thought of everyone coming home made Freya excited. "Maybe we should plan a Welcome Home party for Thomas, Autumn, and Viktor!" she exclaimed. "We can decorate the dock on the lake and get the grill out. Thomas can cook some burgers and dogs." Thrilled, Vita kneeled and whispered, "That's sounds like a great idea! And let us not forget treats like fruit and cupcakes. Oh, yeah, and let's invite some friends."

"We only have a week to plan everything!" said Freya. She paused before continuing in a serious tone, "Why does Jaquan only come home at night?" She hoped her question did not ruin their joyful moment. The silence lingered for several seconds before Vita answered, "Jaquan has been distraught since Jada left home. He is convinced that she is dead and buried in the woods somewhere on the property. Ever since this past December, he has been going into the woods looking for her. We tried everything to stop him, I even showed him Jada's note. But in his mind, Jada did not run away. So, he comes into the house at night and lurks around. But don't worry, he will never harm you." Freya questioned, "Do you believe that Jada ran away?"

Vita stopped combing Freya's hair. She was not sure that she believed her daughter ran away, even after Autumn showed her the letter, along with Jada's diary. It contained entries that Jada was unhappy and was planning to leave. Vita continued to monitor Jada's credit card and there was no activity since she disappeared. Assuming her daughter ran away was better than accepting she was dead.

"That is what Autumn told me, and it was written in Jada's journal. I cannot believe she was unhappy. I was sure we were close. She told me everything. I don't understand why or what happened. I just hope she is safe and sound somewhere and she will be back some day."

They switched places. Now Freya combed Vita's hair. Vita began to cry as she stared into nowhere. "What if Jaquan is right and my baby is dead out there on the estate? What if she was trying to run away and never made it off the property!" spoke Vita, wiping her tears.

"I am sorry to upset you. I just wanted to know," Freya comforted. Vita grabbed one of Freya's hands. "It's fine. I am relieved to be able to talk with someone about it. Every time I want to talk about Jada, everyone scatters. Thank you, Freya. You are the best thing that has happened to me in months." She pulled her around to face her. "I have been thinking about something especially important for a few weeks now. At this moment, I am more than certain that I want to ask you this." She wiped her tears and asked, "Would you allow me to adopt you?"

It did not take Freya long to say, "Yes!" She didn't see herself anywhere else. But her happiness turned to sadness when she thought about what she did to her own mother. "Vita, are you sure you want to adopt me? I did something very bad." Freya looked away both afraid and ashamed about what she was going to reveal. Vita gave her a questioning glance. Freya continued, "You see, my mother used to treat me badly. My life was miserable. She would beat me, make me do things with drug dealers in exchange for drugs. When she came home from her binges, I was her personal butler. One time I was pregnant. She had no money for an abortion and did not want anyone to know so she beat it out of me. After that, I vowed to kill my mother. So, I put poison in her sandwich, and she died. That is how I ended up here with you."

She knew the vital information could jeopardize her freedom and new home, but she felt Vita deserved the truth if she was considering adopting her. Vita shook her head. "Honey, you didn't kill your mother. Now her death was suspicious, but I have a friend in the Homicide Unit. We reviewed the documentation about the case. Your mother died of a drug overdose." She stood up from the chair and gestured for Freya to follow her. They entered the office. Vita walked around the desk and took a seat. She handed her the death certificate and pointed at the bottom. *Cause of death: Drug overdose.* Freya felt lightheaded and took a seat in the chair. Vita walked over to the same side and leaned on the desk. "You're not a killer."

Freya thought back to the day she removed the sandwich from her mother's suite. She tried to remember things that she may have missed on that day. Suddenly, the vision of the untouched sandwich invaded her thoughts. She was so nervous about her mother being dead, she didn't notice that her mother never ate any of the sandwich that she had discarded in her school dumpster. Vita went back to the other side of the desk, allowing Freya to process for a few seconds before continuing, "If my mother were abusing me, I probably would have tried the same thing. So, what is your answer? Do you want me to be your mom? I would love to have a smart little firecracker like you around for good." She displayed a smile.

Freya gathered herself. "I would be honored to be your daughter." She stood and walked around the desk to hug Vita.

Unexpectedly, their warm moment was disturbed by someone entering the office. When Freya looked up, she was startled at the tall, fair skinned man with immature facial hair on his face. His hair was light sandy brown, course, and in desperate need of a trim. A splitting image of his father. He wore a dingy grey long sleeve shirt and camouflage pants that hugged his slim physic. His tan Timberland boots were laced all the way up to the top.

"Freya, this is Jaquan," said Vita. She approached her stepson and tried to embrace him, but he stood back. It wasn't that he did not like Vita; the young man had abandonment issues and showing love and affection was not his strong point. "I am going to take a shower. Could you make me something to eat?"

Vita nodded and turned to Freya. "Well, you wanted to meet Jaquan in person so there you go. Come on, let's go to the kitchen. I always keep his favorite food in the house for these moments." She gestured for Freya who hurried behind her. In the kitchen, Freya giggled when she saw that Jaquan's favorite food was simply pizza rolls. She could not believe that with all the options he had, pizza rolls were his number one choice. Vita knew exactly what Freya was thinking.

"I know, pizza rolls of all the things he would call his favorite. But Jaquan has always been a simple person, and I have always loved that about him. He did not care about the latest fashions or being popular. He loves nature and feeds off people's energy." She placed the pizza rolls in the oven.

"Do you worry about Jaquan staying in the woods all day and night?" questioned Freya.

"I used to worry. But Jaquan is a Boy Scout, and he has extensive training with the Military Elite Program. He can survive a winter in the woods. Also, we have a solar powered bunker, and I know he uses it. I have a groundkeeper that goes out there and stocks it up with water, non-perishable items, and other necessities twice a month. Jaquan uses the bare minimum." Vita said, giving Freya a clever look. Fifteen minutes later, the timer went off for the pizza rolls. Jaquan entered the kitchen. Freya and Vita sat at the island and discussed their plans for the barbeque. Jaquan ate in silence.

Once Jaquan finished his food, he put his plate inside the sink, washed his hands, and turned from the sink. "Nice meeting you, Freya. You remind me of my younger sister." He smiled and walked out the back door, heading to the woods.

Vita ran to the back door and yelled, "Please, come to the cookout this coming weekend! Your father will be home, and he is grilling food!"

CAN OF WORMS

Finally, the weekend! Everyone was home. Thomas was in full "man of the house" mode as he flipped the burgers on the grill. He was rocking back and forth to his oldies playlist that played a couple of feet from the grill. This was the first time in months he was able to be at home and relax with his family. He had so much to celebrate. Bloomfield Inc had landed a billion-dollar investor, and it was up from here. Now, majority of his business matters could be conducted from his home. This meant he would be able to spend more time with his family and get to know Freya more. He missed Jada but he knew for a fact that she was alive, it was just a matter of finding her. By his side at the grill was his wife holding the tray with one hand, while waving smoke away with the other. Freya, Autumn, and Viktor sat in their chairs, enjoying the view of the lake while conversing.

"My grandfather owned all this land and had this manmade lake made for his family to enjoy. One day, I will enjoy this very same lake as I watch my children run around and play," spoke Autumn. She took a sip of her wine. Viktor rolled his eyes. "Wait a minute, honey! How do you know you will inherit the estate to raise your family!" Autumn released a wicked laugh before replying, "Boy, what! You plan on squeezing a baby out through your little penis? Just leave the baby making to me please." Viktor countered, "Heffa! Times have changed. We are in the twenty-first century where same sex couples can grow their family. I will adopt just like we are doing Freya."

Freya observed Autumn rubbing her belly and questioned, "How many children do you want to have?" Before Autumn could answer, Vita interrupted, "Everyone, I have an announcement to make." She kissed her husband before addressing her family and friends. "I would like to announce that we will be adopting Freya! And in the next few weeks, she will become an official Bloomfield!" The family huddled around Freya giving her hugs and kisses as everyone clapped. Strangers approached Freya showing love, welcoming her to the family. Autumn and Viktor started dancing silly causing people to laugh. From the outside looking in the Bloomfield's was the idea of the perfect family.

Vita went inside and returned with a vanilla cake with whipped buttercream icing. The name *Freya Bloomfield* was written on the cake in bright pink. She placed it in the center of the table. Thomas announced it was time to eat. Everyone joined hands and he led prayer. Afterwards, people shuffled around helping themselves to the food on the table. Freya got her plate and found a seat at one of the tables. Baked beans, corn on the cob, grilled shrimp, grilled chicken, and steak fitted her large plate. Viktor came and took a seat across from her. He slid over a bowl of pasta salad before winking at her. Freya loved Vita's pasta salad; how could she have forgotten to pile that on her plate? The two dug in. While eating, Freya overheard a couple women chatting at the table behind her.

"They are truly the perfect family! Jada is missing all of this. I heard she was traveling the world volunteering on a project that helps the less fortunate." Freya wondered why Vita and Thomas were telling people that Jada was traveling when she was missing. The discussion reignited her suspicion about who was responsible for Jada's disappearance. She drifted off and began thinking about various scenarios of what could have happened to Jada and why.

"Hey, Freya, are you okay?" Viktor asked. Freya snapped out of her daze just in time to notice Thomas going into the house with a tray of cooked burgers. She then noticed Autumn hurrying inside the house, appearing to have to go pee. She answered Viktor, "I am okay. I just can't believe I am going to be a Bloomfield." Viktor waved his fork, his mouth full of food. "Well, you better get used to it because we locked in now." They both laughed.

Once Autumn was inside, she slowed her pace down and entered the kitchen where Thomas was at the counter. He was whistling while preparing the last of the burgers for the grill. She took a moment taking all of him in. A simple navy-blue t-shirt complimented his well-defined muscles, the matching cargo shorts that hung off his hips perfectly, it was clear he had been hitting the gym a lot lately. He looked so relaxed sporting his favorite leather slip in slides. Autunm sucked her lips; damn he was sexy. She looked out the window to ensure everyone was still on the dock before announcing her pregnancy to him. Thomas turned away from the counter quickly, displaying a shocked look on his face when he saw Autumn standing there. He looked around to make sure no one was around before demanding her to get an abortion. His words hurt and Autumn began to cry. "What do you mean get rid of it? We are going to be a family one day, and children are in our plan!" She grabbed another bottle of wine from the cabinet.

Thomas took a deep breath to calm himself down. "Autumn, we cannot have children. In fact, I want all of this to end today. Why would you think it's okay to have a baby by your mother's husband? This is not a VC Andrews novel, get a grip. Like I told you before, it was a mistake, and I love Vita." He picked up the tray of burgers and headed outside to the grill, leaving her alone in the kitchen. Autumn was livid. She could not believe that the two-year affair with her stepfather had come to this. The rejection hurt, especially with two babies growing inside of her. She gathered herself, opened the bottle of wine and returned to the dock.

Neither she nor Thomas noticed that Jaquan was lurking in the shadows, eating one of the burgers. He could not believe what he was hearing, but it confirmed what Jada had confided in him before she went missing. He was now more than sure that Autumn was responsible for his sister's disappearance. He remembered hearing Vita talking about her grandfather building multiple bunkers on the property, but he needed the original blueprint to find out how many were originally on the estate. He grabbed some of the extra burgers and headed out into the woods again. He planned to use one of his contacts to retrieve the original plans and not return until he found Jada.

Outside, everyone continued to enjoy good food, drinks, and music. "Damn, that food was so good. I love when Thomas is home because he cooks a lot," said Viktor, taking a drink of his wine. "I am excited as well. I have been missing having a little sister around," added Autumn, returning her stare to the lake. "I am happy to be here with the both of you! I would have never thought that I would go from foster care to being adopted by a loving family," responded Freya, taking a sip of wine.

Autumn stole a stare at Thomas who was sitting at one of the tables with Vita. He was all over her mother as if they were in love. Her heart burned with envy as she witnessed the happy couple finishing each other's sentences and displaying affection. The unhappily married man no longer existed. She remembered the first time she and Thomas were together. She was at her new college in North Carolina for a week and he was in town for a business event. She was having issues with adjusting to being away from home. The moment she found out he was in town for business, she contacted him, and they met for dinner. After dinner, they spent the evening talking. Autumn expressed that she was home sick. The more they laughed and drank, the more appealing Thomas became to her. She began to lust as she listened to her stepfather explain different methods of coping with separation.

The man she had despised and ignored for years was arousing her. The tone of his deep smooth voice made her throb between her legs. His freshly cut hair and trimmed goatee complimented his full lips. She imagined him kissing her with them on every inch of her body. She allowed her eyes to roam to his chest; admiring his well-defined muscles that seemed to stand out more than before through his dress shirt. As she continued to lust, Thomas instructed her to order more drinks before going to the men's room. He was happy that he and Autumn were bonding. As he walked away his stepdaughter watched him. When he was out of sight, she waved their waitress over and ordered another round. The waitress returned with two shots of rum. Autumn thanked her and used her credit card to pay the tab.

Now she had to figure out how to get Thomas in his hotel bed before he went home the following evening. Then, she remembered that she had a powder substance from her friend Levi. She took it out of her purse and poured it in his drink. By the time he returned, the substance had dissolved. She watched him drink and anticipated the events that would follow.

An hour later, Thomas admitted that he was too drunk to drive back to his hotel, so Autumn drove him. Once they made it inside his hotel room, she wasted no time seducing him. The substance did not affect Thomas's performance as he hallucinated. In his eyes, he was making love to his wife who had flown in to surprise him. But reality struck the next morning when he awakened with Autumn in his arms. Frantic, he hurried and dressed as Autumn sat at the foot of the bed. She was satisfied because Thomas had stroked her so good she could never let him go. He vowed to never do it again and even considered telling Vita about the mistake. But Autumn was not letting go that easily, she managed to convince him that Vita would not accept him fucking her daughter. She promised to keep the secret if he made sure he came more frequently to spend time with her.

As time passed, Autumn wanted more than just wining, dining, and sex. She wanted a relationship and children. Thomas was trapped and found himself going with Autumn's flow more. But in the back of his mind, he tried to figure out how to break things off. He hoped that Autumn would fall for a man in college and no longer want him. He even tried performing poorly sexually, but he had to admit the young girl had the ability to sexually stimulate him well. He had fallen weak many times for her flesh, but he loved his wife more than getting his dick wet. The more time went by, the harder it would get to break away.

When Jada came up missing, Thomas sat back and questioned why. Did his daughter receive karma for his sins? He decided from that point to do right by his family in hopes his daughter would return safely. He could not take back everything he had done in the past, but he could start doing right moving forward. The first thing on his agenda was to break it off with Autumn. He knew it would risk her telling Vita, but he would trust God in it all. He would enjoy every single moment with his family moving forward, because once things hit the fan, he could possibly lose them.

Snapping back to the present time, Autumn left the celebration and retreated to her suite. She sat on her balcony and watched everyone from afar while dialing Levi. He answered on the first ring. Wiping her tears, Autumn spoke, "Friend! Can you fucking believe this bastard told me to abort our babies!" Levi used his ear and shoulder to hold the cell in place. "Bitch, what! There is no way he has been fucking you all this time and suddenly has a change of heart. Oh, wait, scratch that! He is just doing what the average man does! Friend, I told you to stop dropping those panties for him a long time ago." Levi swung the chair around so that his client could see the style. Satisfied, she paid him, and Levi removed the cape still listening to Autumn. "He is on the dock with my mother acting like they are in love again. He must be low on money." She tried to convince herself that he still wanted her.

"Girl, you know it's all about the money. If you need to get away from everything, you know I have an extra suite," said Levi, waving his next client over to the shampoo bowl. Autumn focused on Thomas and answered, "I don't know what to do, Levi. I just can't believe this is happening. But if I can't deal, I will see you sooner than later." She ended the call. After another hour of enduring the affection between Thomas and Vita, she got sleepy and retreated to her bed.

LAW OF NATURE

"Mrs. Bloomfield, congratulations! You are pregnant!" said the doctor, giving her the slip of paper revealing her blood test results. Vita sat in the office chair in shock for minutes, trying to process what she just heard. After several seconds of silence, the doctor grew concerned. "Are you okay, Vita? Do you need water?"

"Um, I'm fine. It's just that after Jada, I thought I could no longer have any children. Thomas and I tried a couple of years ago, and it failed. Forgive me. I'm stunned and don't know what to do with a baby at my age, and I just adopted Freya." Vita got up, grabbed her Celine bag, then exited the exam room. After rushing down the gloomy hall, she stopped at the door to the waiting area. She tried to gather herself before pushing the door open.

In the waiting area, Freya and Viktor were preoccupied by their phones, not noticing her. "You guys hungry? I know a great coffee shop a couple blocks away that serves great food." She avoided making eye contact as she hurried out the entrance. Viktor and Freya gave each other a look of confusion before following. By the time they made it out the entrance, Vita was halfway to her car. It was early but already too hot for Viktor to stand it, so he jogged to the car. Freya was on his heels. When they entered, Vita had the air conditioner blasting. Concerned, Viktor questioned as he buckled his seatbelt, "Are you okay, mom? You look flushed." Vita answered, placing the gear in drive, "I just need to eat and drink something cool. You know this August heat can be unbearable at times for me." She drove out of the parking lot.

Freya remembered hearing Vita in the bathroom that morning throwing up and was sure she was pregnant. Thomas had been spending a lot of time around the house. He and Vita were getting it in. Some days no one saw them because they stayed in their suite. Thomas was also spending time with the children. Freya had witnessed Jaquan having breakfast with his father in the wee hours of the morning. Thomas was also spending time with Freya and Viktor, teaching them how to shoot out in the woods. He was even displaying his great cooking skills. Everyone was enjoying Thomas's presence except for Autumn. She began to isolate herself from the family and would be seen either coming or going. She even postponed her returned to college, telling her mother that she needed time to make sure she was going down the right path.

Worried, Freya would go into Autumn's suite to bring her food and sit with her while she laid in bed depressed. She would not share details on what was bothering her. She just told Freya that her heart had been broken. Seeing his sister in such a bad state, Viktor convinced Vita to enroll him in Harmon Private School so that he could be home. He also tried to talk to his sister and find out what was wrong, but Autumn revealed nothing. So, Freya and Viktor continued to check on Autumn daily until one day she stopped coming home.

At the coffee shop, Viktor and Freya sat across from Vita and watched her scarf down her larger than usual lunch. She shoveled the fried potatoes into her mouth like she had not eaten in a week, not paying them any mind. Freya retrieved the pen from the table and wrote on a napkin. She then slid the napkin to Viktor. When he opened it up, it read: *She is pregnant!* Viktor used the napkin to wipe his mouth before taking a drink of his water with lemon. He would not be surprised that his mother was pregnant the way she and

Thomas were spending a lot of time together. Viktor leaned over to Freya and whispered, "Well, I am happy for mom. It's like our family is coming back together." He nudged Freya playfully, taking a bite of his chicken sausage. Freya nodded in agreement and focused back on her food. She was happy for Vita and was excited to become a big sister in the future.

At Levi's apartment, Autumn sat in the middle of the living room with her legs crossed Indian style. Her eyes were closed as she smoked a joint and enjoyed a glass of wine.

"So, when are you going to break the news to your mother that you are carrying her husband's buns in the oven?" Levi questioned, sitting on the couch polishing his fingernails.

Autumn opened her eyes. "I plan to before Christmas. Thomas is in denial about us, and I am patiently waiting for him to come around. But if he does not man up, I will take the driver seat." She took another sip of wine. Since revealing her pregnancy, Thomas was giving her the cold shoulder. He even went as far as canceling the lease to the condo they shared. He paid movers to pack up all her belongings and place them in storage. She had no idea what was happening until Thomas slid the storage key under her suite door a couple of weeks ago.

"Friend, you know what you need to do! Shit, go home and break that happy family up like I taught you! Fuck waiting for Christmas!" suggested Levi. He began blowing his freshly polished nails. Autumn agreed, "Friend, you are right! Thomas is not throwing me away without a fight. All the shit I have gone through to set things up for us to be together! Hell, I even went as far as replacing Jada so that mother could be ready for the big blow," explained Autumn.

Levi displayed a vacant stare. "Damn, I forgot about your ruthless ass. I cannot believe you have that little girl thinking she killed her own mother when you know you gave her those bad drugs! I remember Catherine when I was a kid growing up. She used to hang with Jaquan's mother Samantha and this other woman named Anika. Catherine was the youngest, so they looked after her. Then one day Anika just disappeared, and shit seemed to go downhill. Samantha killed herself and Catherine turned to drugs. I think Anika got killed by one of her johns because she was a prostitute." Autumn did not care about that as she continued, "Well, her Uncle Kareem was in on it too. Man, his old ass had some moves in the bedroom. And can you believe that my pussy was not good enough payment? I had to apply for a credit card in my name and max it out to pay him $10,000.00 to let Freya go to foster care!" She whined, refilling her glass.

Levi pointed. "You always had a thing for older men. But make sure that when you blow the Bloomfield residence up, just make sure I get a front row seat." Little did they both know that opportunity was coming sooner than later.

Autumn laughed before noticing a text from Viktor. The text read, "Thomas is cooking a special dinner tonight and he is going to be making an important announcement." She displayed a devilish grin before replying to the text. *Okay.* She looked at Levi. "Well, do you have any plans tonight? Because I will not let another family announcement happen without me making mines." She tossed the keys to her Audi to Levi.

Levi was not catching anything until his nails were dry, so he watched the keys fall on his lap. "Now, wait a minute before you go crashing a party! Are you sure those little bundles of joy don't belong to anyone else? Like Kareem?"

Autumn playfully whispered, "And who cares who the babies belong to? These are Thomas's babies. Besides, Kareem's old dried-up ass sperm not marching anywhere." She displayed a look of disgust. They both shared a laugh. They continued smoking weed and drinking wine, waiting for the explosion that would happen later that evening. Thoughts danced in Autumn's mind about how everyone would react. The dinner tonight would be epic at the Marchbanks Estate. For a moment, she felt bad for Freya, Vita, and Viktor. But making Thomas's life miserable had become her new obsession.

Instead of going home after brunch, Vita, Viktor, and Freya spent hours shopping before making it home that evening. As everyone put their shopping bags away, Thomas and Jaquan waited for them in the den with dinner already prepared. It had been several months since Jaquan sat at the dinner table with his family. But after some convincing from his father, he was willing to try under the conditions that Autumn would not be there. But his conditions were now voided. Because while everyone put their bags away and freshened up for dinner, Levi was outside parking. He exited the driver's seat and walked to the passenger side to open the door. Autumn stepped out and looked up at the Marchbanks Estate. She smiled, ready to ruin Thomas's life. They entered and walked through the sitting area to the dining room. Thomas and Jaquan were now at the dining room table having small talk.

"Mr. Bloomfield, I brought a plus one for dinner tonight. I hope you don't mind," she said, taking a seat at the end of the dining room table. "Greetings, everyone," spoke Levi, taking a seat next to her.

When Jaquan laid eyes on Autumn and Levi, he stood at his feet. He instantly exited the dining room, headed out of the door, and back into the woods. Thomas sighed and took a drink of his wine. He knew that it would be a long night as he stared at the two uninvited guests at the other end of the table. There was no point in trying to talk Autumn out of it. The day he had dreaded was now front and center. He could only hope that he did not lose his family after this.

Once everyone was at the table, Thomas led grace, then everyone began to eat. For several minutes, everyone ate in silence enjoying the food. Autumn scarfs the food on her plate down before going for seconds. She missed Thomas's cooking. Levi was enjoying the food, but he was thirstier for the drama, so he took it upon himself to break the awkward silence. "Mr. Bloomfield, you can burn in the kitchen! Can I take a doggy bag?" Thomas gave Levi a stern look. "Thank you for the compliment. I had a large family, so we had to cook. I have tried to pass my skills down to one of my children, but I guess no one cared to learn." Seeing an opportunity, Levi nudged Autumn who opened her mouth to speak. Instead, Vita spoke, "Well, baby don't speak too soon. You may get another chance to pass your great cooking skills down because ... I'm pregnant!" She announced.

Freya and Viktor looked at each other and smiled, while Levi and Autumn looked at each other in shock. Thomas dropped his fork, grabbed Vita's hand, then began kissing it. "Baby, I love you and I look forward to our new child. This could not be a more perfect time." He looked at Vita. "Let's renew our vowels, especially since the adoption has been finalized with Freya. Our family is growing, and we have so much to celebrate."

"Aw, hell nah! He did not do that!" mumbled Levi, taking a drink of his water. Viktor and Freya got up and went to hug Vita. Autumn stared daggers into Thomas. He gave her a smirk. Game on. Autumn never broke her stare while using a fork to tap her wine glass. "Attention, family. I have an especially important announcement to make." When everyone focused their attention, she continued, "I am also pregnant with twins!" She never took her eyes off Thomas. His light skin turned red as he tried to conceal his anger. She blew him a kiss and concluded, "Thomas, looks like you will have three more tries instead of one." She took a drink of her wine. Levi grabbed one of the open bottles of wine and refilled his glass, while Freya and Viktor looked at each other in confusion.

Viktor needed clarification on what he had just heard. "Autumn, why would you say that to Thomas?" While Viktor was trying to figure out if his ears were deceiving him, Freya began to think back, and it all made sense. Autumn was fine when her mother and stepfather were not getting along; however, she seemed to be upset when they grew closer over the summer. Freya also remembered when they both went inside the day of the barbeque. It seemed like

Autumn's attitude changed and she had been different ever since.

Autumn observed the various expressions of shock and confusion, so she clarified, "Well, for anyone who has not caught on, I am pregnant with Thomas babies!" At that point, Vita's face was mortified; she could not believe what she was hearing.

"Yeah, that's right, mother. I am pregnant with your husband's twins. While you two have been prancing around here like one big happy family, I have been having an affair with him since I started college. We had plans to get married and be together. He was supposed to be waiting for the right time to break the news to you! But I don't think there will be one, so I am taking the cat out the bag now." Vita looked at her husband. He was too busy still staring at Autumn, who now had the smirk on her face. He addressed Autumn through gritted teeth. "I told you to get rid of them. I even scheduled the appointment." Vita started feeling sick to her stomach. She scooted her seat from the table, stood up, and exited the dining area. She made it to her private bathroom and released what she had eaten into the toilet.

In the dining room, Thomas pounded his fist on the table. He yelled, "You vindictive bitch! You were not happy until you broke my marriage up! I told you I didn't want you, nor the babies. You just refuse to take 'no' for an answer!"

"Well, you are the one who decided it was okay to fuck me and hold a two-year relationship!" Autumn fired back. Thomas yelled again, "That was a mistake! You know we were drunk! And remember that I only continued because you threatened to tell everyone!" He hurried out of the dining room to check on his wife. Freya and Viktor sat at the table in silence while Levi continued his meal, finding the show amusing. Satisfied, Autumn retreated to her suite to grab a few things. She knew that after tonight, she probably would never step foot onto the Marchbanks Estate until her mother died. With the silence, everyone could hear Thomas and Vita yelling at each other from their suite. "Damn, this is like an episode of *The Haves and the Have Nots*!" said Levi, finishing up his meal. Once his plate was clean, he grabbed the unopened bottle of wine, stood up, then exited the dining room. He met Autumn coming down the stairs with a duffle bag. They exited the house, got into her car, and left.

Still in shock, Freya and Viktor cleaned up and retreated to Freya's suite. They listened to their parents argue for hours before Thomas retreated to one of the guest suites. That night, Freya tossed and turned thinking about what happened at dinner. She knew the family was not perfect but had no idea things were this messy. But she had to think rationally and evaluate all the red flags she was dismissing because of how glamorous things were. The Bloomfield's had a missing child that they appeared to be moving on without except for Jaquan, who spent his days in the woods searching. Viktor was enrolled in boarding school when she first came and it was never clear why. Autum and Thomas were having an affair, while Vita walked around as if everything was perfect. And with all that they decided to adopt a child.

But despite all of that, Freya still reassured herself that she wanted to stay. She ventured downstairs to the kitchen and drunk a glass of wine before returning to her suite and falling asleep.

 WINTER

It was now winter and the Marchbanks Estate had been quiet since the explosion at dinner weeks ago. Vita stayed in her suite most of the time, only coming out for doctors' appointments. The family should have been celebrating Thanksgiving. Months before, Viktor and Freya had plans to surprise the family with a holiday dinner. But Autumn's announcement dampened everything. So, they decided to go into the inner city and pick up some barbeque from a well-known spot located in downtown Kansas City. When they made it home, they took the barbeque platter, napkins, plates, ginger ale, and bottle waters into Vita's suite where she laid on the couch depressed. The food seemed to cheer her up and they spent the evening watching movies and eating the barbeque.

"Home Alone is my favorite movie!" said Viktor, resting his head on his mother's knee. Freya took a bite of the tinder rib. She savored the flavor before speaking with her mouth full, "I have never seen this movie before. My Uncle Kareem was too cheap so we never had cable unless it was connected

illegally. But the cable company would always find out about it around Christmas and disconnect it." Vita shook her head. "I can't believe they left him at home. I would have been terrified." Freya smiled and placed her free hand on Vita's belly and the baby kicked. "Mother, what are you going to name my little brother or sister?" questioned Viktor, never taking his eyes off the television. Vita sighed, "I don't know. I honestly haven't thought about it. But I have an idea! Why don't you two come up with a boy name and a girl name and then we will see which ones are the best."

"Deal!" said Viktor, grabbing the notepad and pen from the table. They laughed as they watched Viktor write down names on the note pad. He looked up at them and spoke in a joking manner, "Okay, you two are laughing now, but one of the names on this pad is the winner!" Suddenly, everyone was disturbed by Thomas entering. When Vita looked at him, her laughter turned to anger. Viktor and Freya exited the suite, taking the movie night to Freya's suite.

Annoyed, Vita yelled, "What do you want, Thomas! Did we not discuss space!" She positioned herself on the edge of the couch. She reached for one of the pieces of turkey on the platter. "Vita, we need to talk and not scream over one another. I am not going anywhere until we come to some type of arrangement so that I can be a part of this pregnancy and my new child's life." He grabbed one of the ribs and took a bite. "I was drunk and things happened. I tried to get out, but she held that shit over my head for two years. She was not taking 'no' for an answer and threatened to tell you. I could not take it anymore, so I just stopped things. And just like I predicted, she blew the household up because I rejected her. I know this may sound arrogant, but come on, Vita, let's move on and get through this, especially for our new baby. This is not the end of us and you know this. I am willing to walk through your fury of fire and wait for you to feel comfortable with me again. But I am not leaving!"

Vita looked at her husband and continued chewing her food. The man that stood before her slept with her daughter. In the real world that was grounds for a divorce. But Vita had to remember all the things she and Thomas had been through. They held secrets that bonded them, and she had to admit they were responsible for things far worse than what was going on. She had to face reality; he did not walk out on her when she was at her worse. He endured and accepted things that the average person would not. At that moment, she realized that no matter how messed up things were, she and Thomas were built to weather the storms together.

"You are right, Thomas. We certainly are bonded by many secrets. So, we need to stay together. But I am disappointed that when we finally get out of the woods with the old shit, you light the fire again and complicate things. How could you fall weak to her flesh? You were able to keep it together with her mother years ago. Now, we must go back into the past and clean some shit up to work through what's happening now. And let's not forget more children to raise," she spoke, picking up a rib from the tray.

Thomas snatched the rib from her hand and took a bite. "I am glad you said that because I wasn't going anywhere anyway. And take those green contacts out of your eyes; I no longer want a reminder of Autumn." He stared at her for several minutes with a serious look. The look reminded her of when she met him at an after-hour spot in the inner city years before they married. He was the forbidden fruit in her life and allowed her to channel her wild side. She remembered sneaking away from her husband, Samuel, to be with him before she had children.

When Vita was having infertility problems, Thomas was her support system through it all. Her late husband Samuel made it clear that if she could not have a baby, that he would soon divorce her. The stipulations of her marriage placed a lot of pressure on her, causing her to have high-risk pregnancies that resulted in miscarriages. She had a best friend named Anika that she met when they were in high school. They were close despite their different lives. Vita was raised in privilege, while Anika raised herself in the rough streets of Kansas City. Venturing into adulthood, Anika and Vita went their separate ways for a while. However, years later, they reconnected after Vita began experiencing marriage issues. Anika had become a drug addicted prostitute and one of Thomas's bottom hoes. But despite Anika's lifestyle she was a loyal friend to Vita and money could never buy that. That's why what happened to Anika would always haunt both Vita and Thomas.

Vita allowed the memories of the night that Anika died invade her mind. She would never forget how sore she was after giving birth to a stillborn. Another failed pregnancy would be the death of her marriage. She dreaded Samuel coming home from his business trip. This time, she would welcome her husband home with a new daughter even if she had to steal a baby from the nursery. She spent hours in the hospital contemplating which baby she would take. Then her cell rang, it was Thomas. He informed her that Anika was in labor and refusing to go to a local hospital. Vita instructed Thomas to come pick her up from the hospital. Less than an hour later, he parked in front of the emergency room and Vita got inside. In the back seat, Anika was laying down trying to endure the pain.

Vita forgot about her issues and began trying to convince Anika to go inside the hospital. But despite the pain, she still refused in fear that child protective services would take her daughter. They headed over to Kansas City, Kansas to go to a hospital that was not aware of Anika's history. But on the way, Anika needed to push. Vita climbed in the backseat and while Thomas drove, she helped Anika deliver her baby. After giving birth, Anika only lived long enough to hold her baby and name her Autumn. When she took her last breath, Thomas pulled over onto the side of the road and turned the car off. Vita would never forget the dead silence as she sat there holding Autumn. Anika wanted Vita to take care of her baby if something ever happened to her.

Now Vita had a plan. Anika's delivery and unfortunate death would become Vita's ticket to keep her late husband. Instead of going to the hospital, Anika and Thomas went to the Marchbanks Estate. They burned Thomas's car with Anika in the back seat. Afterwards, Vita was able to retrieve some of Anika's cremains before they pushed the charcoaled car into the lake. Tired, Vita went and checked into a hotel for a couple days to rest and bond with her new baby. By the time Samuel came home, Vita had a fake birth certificate and was welcoming him home to a new baby. Autumn was now Vita's daughter and her marriage was no longer on the rocks. But only Thomas and Vita would know about the charcoaled car sitting at the bottom of the lake on the Marchbanks Estate. Vita was saddened about what happened to Anika. But she learned to move on and raised Autumn like she was her own and was able to ignore the truth. However, at this moment, that all changed because the true Anika shined through her daughter.

Snapping out of her thoughts, Vita stood up and walked into the bathroom. She washed her hands before removing the green contacts from her eyes. She no longer needed the contacts because Autumn was officially not her daughter.

When she exited the bathroom, Thomas waited for her on the couch. "Now, that's the Vita I met years ago looking for trouble. Of course, without the small pudge in her stomach." Thomas tried to joke with his wife.

"Remember when Anika tried to sleep with you? Well, this situation reminds me of that. I can't believe Viktor and Freya had to witness that dysfunctional shit at the table that night. And Autumn's friend looks familiar," said Vita. Thomas palmed his head. "Yeah, unfortunately, that familiar face is little Levi. I didn't bring it up because I didn't want Viktor, Freya, or even Jaquan to witness that. They should never see those sides of us. But we are going to erase this situation like we did Anika. I messed up badly and I want to fix it. But we must start by being honest with our children so that they won't doubt us. Because if they stop trusting us, then they will start digging and allow others into our circle like Autumn."

Vita joined Thomas on the couch. She picked up her phone and called her credit card company. "Yes, this is Vita Bloomfield. I would like to cancel one of my black cards immediately, the one ending with 1980." She picked up one of the pickles from the tray while waiting for the representative to confirm that the card was cancelled. After disconnecting the call she questioned, "What are you going to do about those two babies in her belly?" Thomas responded, "We will have to ride her out in court, take them, be done with it." Ready to relax, he went to the bathroom to shower, and Vita followed. She leaned against the sink as her husband showered. "I really don't want this information out. You know the media will have a field day with this! It's already bad enough that I don't know where my daughter is. Have you heard anything from the private investigator?" she inquired.

"The investigator checks in with me every two days. He still has not found anything, but I know Jada is alive. And when it comes to Autumn, we have people in high places that will erase this shit. Our move depends on Autumn's move. If she presses, we press harder. If things go the way I want, we will disassociate her from our family, starting with destroying that fake birth certificate. Anika's death would have to be revealed and I have some people in homicide that will do that. I plan to handle Levi personally," he replied, lathering himself with soap.

"That sounds like a plan. But I feel horrible inside because I raised her as my own. I feel it's only fair that she knows her mother after all this is over." She allowed the tears to fall from her eyes. Thomas exited the shower, wrapped the towel around his waist, then held her in his arms. He ensured her it would be okay. Vita looked into her husband's eyes. "How are you so sure that Jada is alive?"

Thomas planted a kiss on her forehead. "Because I can feel her heartbeat every second of the day." He held out his wrist, displaying a band. Vita questioned, "What is that?" "Remember when I went overseas years ago to invest in this cloning company? Well, they were creating various devices to help loved ones stay connected. This device was in its early stage of development, so the tracking portion of the model was not developed during that time. I thought the device was neat in the stage it was because it allows you to always feel your loved one's heartbeat. When I invested, the company gave me a pair. When Jada saw it, she thought it was cool, so I gave the other one to her. She has never taken it off and her heart is still beating."

Vita began crying uncontrollably while trying to speak, "How do you know this is her heartbeat?" Thomas smiled.

"Well, it has a trigger that when you take it off, it sends an alert. But we have been having it for so long, I know her heartbeat." He slid the band onto Vita's wrist. "I am sure now that you are wearing it, she will notice the change." Vita stood still, studying the heartbeat get more rapid. Panicking, she took off the band and handed it back to Thomas. "You're right, she probably thinks something is wrong." She slipped the band back on his wrist.

After a couple minutes, Jada's heartbeat was regular again. "She knows my heartbeat. So, let's put it back on you to see if she figures out that I am sharing this with you," he suggested. He slipped the band back on Vita; and his prediction was right. Jada's heartbeat increased, but she then calmed down after a few minutes. Vita stared down at the band on her wrist while walking out the bathroom. Content, she laid down and fell asleep to her daughter's heartbeat. Thomas put on his housecoat and walked through the mansion and checked on everyone before returning to the suite. He joined Vita in the bed, wrapped his arms around her, and whispered in her ear, "I wonder if she can feel the baby's heartbeat and mines while I am holding you." He gave her a kiss before falling asleep.

A NEW YEAR

Freya and Viktor relaxed in the den enjoying wine and cocktail shrimp while watching Freya's favorite reality show. Suddenly, thoughts about the last family dinner invaded Viktor's mind. "I hate to keep bringing it up, but I just can't believe that Autumn and Thomas were having an affair." Freya observed him grab another shrimp off the tray and toss it into his mouth. She could never get used to Viktor's bad habit of smacking while eating. With knowledge of his sexuality, Freya could not help but to feel that everything he did seemed intentional and promiscuous. She shook her judgmental thoughts and spoke, "Yeah, just like Levi said, this shit is like an episode of *The Haves and the Have Nots.*"

Viktor agreed, "No, but really, Freya. I thought Autumn at least told me everything. But now that I think about it, she changed after she went to college. She stopped coming home and when she did, it was only for a couple days while Thomas was in town. Here I was thinking she was just enjoying being an adult away from home with unlimited money. But she was having an affair with our stepfather." He retrieved another piece of shrimp. Freya observed Viktor's face turn sour. He eyeballed the shrimp before tossing it back onto the tray. His emotions were all over the place since finding out about the affair. Freya suggested, "I think we should get some rest." She turned off the television. With no words, Viktor went to his suite, leaving Freya to clean up their mess.

The Next Morning

"I am so sorry, Ms. Covington, but we need to induce you and deliver your babies," the doctor spoke. He stood over Autumn as she laid in the hospital bed staring off into space.

Just a week before, the doctor informed Autumn that the babies died. She was a week shy of her 3rd trimester. Autumn refused to believe both her babies were dead. She left the hospital and returned to Levi's. When learning of the devasting news, Levi spent days trying to convince her to go back to the hospital. Then, one day he came home from work and found Autumn passed out on the kitchen floor. Carrying the dead babies was making Autumn sick, but she did not care because at this point she wanted to die with them.

"Look, doctor, just do what you need to do. She is not in any condition to give you any responses or consent. So just do your job," Levi said. The doctor authorized the induction, and the nurse began administering the Pitocin. For the next several hours, Levi stayed by Autumn's side through the labor and delivery.

While watching Autumn in pain, Levi became furious. This was the second time he had to witness a broken woman because of Thomas. He took Autumn's cell and dialed Thomas's number as he exited the hospital room. The phone rang several times and the voicemail picked up. At the sound of the beep, Levi gave him a piece of his mind.

"You sick bastard! How could you play house with her, then decide to go back home as if nothing happened? You stressed the babies inside of her to death and this is all your fault. I promise you will pay one day for the pain you have caused her. Damn, you don't even pick up her calls or respond to her texts! It's like she never existed. Then, I hear you are back living happy-ever-after with your wife. That bitch ain't shit right along with you! What type of woman would take a nigga back that fucked her daughter!" spat Levi. He marked the message urgent and ended the call before returning to Autumn's side.

At the Marchbanks Estate, Thomas confirmed with the doctor that he would cover the medical expenses for the labor and delivery. He hung the phone up, placed it on the desk in the office, and spoke, "The babies died." Vita sat on the other side of the desk shaking her head. Despite the circumstances, she hated to hear that it happened because she could relate. She remembered holding her stillborn child before donating her baby to medical research. Although the thought of Thomas and Autumn's affair still haunted her thoughts, she was prepared to raise the twin boy and girl as her own. Thomas spoke again, "It's not good news, but it eases the road moving forward." Vita nodded in agreement while rubbing her pregnant belly until her baby kicked. She focused on the band on her wrist. "Jada's heartbeat has been racing all day like she is doing cardio." Concerned, Thomas gestured for Vita to hand him the band. "That's normally in the mornings, not in the evening." While he was slipping the band on his wrist, he heard a disturbance. They exited the office and hurried downstairs. Vita observed Freya standing in the foyer looking towards the family room as if she saw a ghost.

When Vita entered the family room, Jaquan stood there smiling while Viktor was hugging someone. Vita immediately recognized the ring with an Aquamarine birthstone on the soiled hand that caressed Viktor's back. Her heart began to pound loudly like a drum as she made it close enough to recognize her daughter, Jada. She almost lost her breath when she looked into her daughter's dark brown eyes. Jada looked as if she had not taken a bath in months, her once long silky black hair was matted, and she was wearing the same pajamas from the Christmas before last. When Jada saw her mother, she let go of Viktor and ran into her arms yelling, "Mommy!" Once in her mother's arms, she whispered, "I felt your heart beating." They both began crying and lowered to the floor. Thomas hurried over to join them.

Viktor wiped his tears and went into the foyer to get Freya. "Come on, Freya, and meet your sister. It's okay, you are family now," he spoke, taking Freya by the hand. He led her into the family room and approached Jaquan. "Where did you find her?" Before answering, Jaquan gave Viktor a hug and apologized for accusing him of Jada's disappearance. He released his embrace and guided them over so that Freya could formally meet Jada. Everyone huddled on the floor together in front of the fire and listened to Jaquan explain how he found her.

After searching the estate for several months, he managed to locate the original plans of the estate that displayed the original bunkers. Mr. Marchbanks had originally ordered to have all but one of the bunkers destroyed after learning that drifters were living inside of them. There was only supposed to be one remaining bunker that Vita kept cleaned and stocked with non-perishable items. However, there was another bunker at the end of the estate that was not destroyed.

"Oh, my God! The crew said they destroyed all the bunkers but one per my father's orders!" interrupted Vita, attempting to untangle Jada's hair. "That's what I wondered. But my guess is that it was just a lazy crew because the bunker was the last one at the end of the grounds," responded Jaquan. Thomas looked over at Jada and she started explaining what happened the night she disappeared.

"On Christmas Eve night, I saw daddy and Autumn in the laundry room. She was trying to kiss daddy, but he pushed her away. I waited in her suite and when she came in, I confronted her about it. She became angry and knocked me out. When I awakened, I was in a bunker tied up and she was standing over me. She untied my hands and made me write a letter explaining that I ran away from home, along with making entries in my diary expressing that I was unhappy and planning to leave. When she was away at school, she sent someone by to make sure I had water and food. I think it was her friend, Levi. He wore a mask, but I could recognize his walk." She paused and took a drink of water. "Autumn made sure I had books, but no electronics were allowed. I didn't know how or when I was getting out or what would happen to me. Then, she made one last visit to me a while ago and said she was going to have me killed because she found someone to replace me. Since that visit, no more water and food came. Good thing I used the food and water in moderation like Jaquan taught me or I would have never survived." She looked over at Freya who was feeling uncomfortable. Vita caressed her daughter's face and guided her focus back to her. "Baby, we will never replace you. Autumn gave me the letter and journal and I thought you ran away!" She helped her up from the floor. "Come on, let's get you cleaned up. Thomas, please take care of Autumn. She has more than crossed the line." She gestured for Freya to come along.

As soon as the ladies were out of the living room, Thomas gestured to Viktor and Jaquan to take a seat. He took the liberty of pouring them both a glass of scotch from the bar. It was time to place all the cards on the table for his family to understand what happened and why.

He took a drink before explaining everything from the beginning. "Viktor, I met your mother when I used to be on the wrong side of money, running the streets. I remember when she walked into an afterhours spot; everyone was looking at her, but I knew for sure I was going to be the one. Before the night ended we were laughing and talking about everything. A fight broke out and we decided to leave. We went to a local bar I owned with my brother, Clayton, who was killed years ago." Thomas looked over at Jaquan.

"During that time, Jaquan, me and your mother were having some relationship issues and Vita was married to

Samuel. He worked a lot and she was feeling lonely. We ended up spending the night together and from that night moving forward, we never went a day without seeing or at least talking to each other." Thomas took a drink of his scotch. "Despite our separate lives, it was like we still had each other. Then, Vita got pregnant by her husband. But our friendship was strong, and we just accepted each other's lives. I started focusing on my relationship with Samantha and we conceived you. I had plans on marrying your mother and I needed money to pay for the wedding she wanted, so I hit the streets hustling harder. I was dealing drugs and even pimping hoes on the strips. That's when I got reacquainted with Vita's best friend, Anika. She was my bottom bitch and made me a lot of money, even when she got pregnant. She was dedicated until she went into labor in the back seat of my Cadillac." He paused and walked over to the window and took a drink.

"It was crazy when Anika went into labor. It was a cold night in November. Vita had not called me all that day and she was not answering any of my calls. When I finally got in touch with her that night, I told her that Anika was in labor. Vita sounded odd on the phone but I was so focused on

Anika that I did not speak on it. She instructed me to pick her up from the downtown hospital. I drove up to the emergency area and she came outside. When she got into the car, I didn't notice that she had given birth. I demanded Anika to get out of the car and go inside the hospital, but she refused. She said that if she gave birth to her daughter anywhere in Missouri then CPS would take her baby. We headed to a hospital forty-five minutes away in Kansas. But about ten minutes into the drive, she was ready to push. Vita ended up delivering Anika's daughter in the back seat that night. She only got a chance to hold her baby and name her Autumn before dying." Thomas drunk the rest of his scotch and went over to the bar to refill his glass. Jaquan and Viktor's eyes were glued to him, anticipating the rest of the story. After pouring another drink he obliged.

"We pulled over alongside a country road. We sat there for about an hour in silence before Vita told me she gave birth to her baby girl, but she died. She was afraid that her marriage was over with Samuel because they were not able to have any children. At that moment, she came up with the idea to keep Anika's baby as her own. With Anika's body still in the backseat, we drove onto the Marchbanks Estate and burned the car. We retrieved some of Anika's ashes and pushed the car into the lake. We called a cab. Vita got dropped off at a hotel and I went home. By the time Samuel made it back, Vita had already forged a birth certificate and had a home doctor to care for her through her recovery. Two months later when I saw her again, she had green contacts. I asked Vita why she was wearing them, and she told me it was because Autumn's eyes were green, and she didn't want her daughter to feel like she didn't have something like her mother. She even convinced Samuel that she had some type of condition that caused her eyes to change colors and he fell for it." Viktor and Jaquan looked at each other in amazement.

"So, you are saying that Autumn is not my sister? Well, that takes the sickness away of you fucking your stepdaughter!" said Viktor. Vita interrupted, "That's what he is saying and that is why I don't plan on divorcing him." Thomas walked over to Vita. He was sorry about what happened but grateful that it did. He could not imagine continuing the life he was living with Autumn holding something over him. He embraced his wife. Everyone watched them for several seconds before joining in. Well everyone except for Freya. Jada looked back and gestured for Freya to come. She took her into the embrace. "It's going to be great having a sister the same age around." Those words made Freya relaxed and allowed the feeling of love to consume her.

Everyone went into the kitchen and Thomas whipped up one of Jada's favorite meals. Vita contacted the emergency locksmith to change all the locks and update her security access codes. She did not want Autumn to ever have access to the property again. That night, everyone slept in Vita and Thomas's suite. Thomas stayed up watching his family sleep peacefully while gazing out the window at the lake. He could not help but to think about his charcoaled Cadillac at the bottom of it. What if Anika never died. Then he and Vita would have just eventually got together. But that meant that Viktor would not have been born. Despite some disagreements, Thomas loved Viktor as if he was his son and the Bloomfield's would not be the same without his spunk. Then he realized that the journey to this very moment was done the way it needed to be.

Trust God and try to do things as right as possible. When negative things happen, either you allow it to break you or you fight to continue until it's time for you to move on. What happened to his daughter was supposed to break him and his family. But once again the Bloomfield's were not broken, they had weathered another storm and were stronger than before. Even Freya won; she survived a life of abuse and poverty. She was rightfully a Bloomfield. This made Thomas feel even more powerful and protective for his family. He made a vow to never allow anything or anyone to hurt them as long as he lived. Now it was time to tie up some lose ends.

 # BROTHER OF MINE

Levi and Autumn embraced each other in the airport terminal. "I will be over to see you as soon as my vacation starts. I'm going to book the flight tonight!" said Levi. Autumn offered a weak smile; she was still depressed and grieving her losses. However, she would manage by taking Kareem on her new journey of life to keep her company. "Well, I have a three-bedroom overlooking the beach in Jamaica, so come anytime. It would be perfect if you moved with me," she replied before walking away to go through check in.

Levi pointed at Kareem while backing away. "Nigga, you better look out for my girl! She has had a rough time!"

"Hey, you stay on your side of the tracks. I got things over here," responded Kareem, following behind Autumn.

They boarded the plane and settled in their first-class seats. Autumn gazed out the window. They had a one-way trip and could not return to Kansas City. Originally, Autumn preferred to stick around and cause more misery, but when she received a surprised visit from both Vita and Thomas, she had no other choice but to leave. They were generous enough to give her $400,000 to start a new life on the condition that she never showed her face again.

Vita revealed to her that Anika asked her to watch her baby when she was a week old; and was later found dead from a drug overdose in an abandoned house a week later. She gave Autumn the urn with Anika's ashes along with some photos. She hoped that she would feel remorse and mention what she did to Jada. But when she realized that Autumn was not going to say anything, Vita and Thomas informed her that Jada had been found alive and told them the story of what happened. After handling Autumn, Vita and Thomas made a visit to Kareem and informed him how they knew about the role he played in his sister's death. To save himself, Kareem confirmed that Levi started everything. Murder had no statute of limitation so both Kareem and Autumn played it safe and decided to leave the country. After talking to Kareem, Vita remembered Catherine and her younger brother when they were incredibly young. What a coincidence. Anika used to look after them until their grandmother passed away. Catherine and Kareem were placed into foster care because no family would take them. Years passed and by the time Anika found Catherine, she was strung out on crack and in and out of jail. Anika managed to help Catherine get back on track, but when she disappeared, Catherine relapsed.

Shortly after the plane took off, Autumn requested a drink. She was now feeling the reality of how her life was changing. Her plan had failed, and she lost a good family. She desperately wanted to return to her normal life. But now, she was fleeing the country and the only person she kept dear to her heart was Levi, who would be thousands of miles away. She never felt so lonely in her life and the sight of her two dead babies haunted her memory. Then finding out her biological mother was dead made it no better. She would never know who her biological father was because her mother was a prostitute. She looked at the box on her lap that contained her children's ashes and began to cry.

Later that night, Levi entered his apartment and tossed his keys on the counter. After seeing Autumn and Kareem off at the airport, he returned to work to finish up some appointments. After closing, he joined a friend for a couple of drinks before turning in for the night. He turned on some jazz music and went to shower. As the warm water massaged his back, he thought about Autumn. The music serenaded his ears as he talked to himself. "Autumn, baby, I may take you up on your offer." He selected his favorite grapefruit scent body wash and lathered his body. He stood back under the shower head and allowed the warm water to rinse the day away. As he watched the lather going down the drain, he thought about Samantha. She always crossed his mind especially when he was in the bathroom. He stepped out of the shower, dried himself off, put on his robe, then went to the kitchen.

He opened the Musigny bottle of wine that Autumn took from the wine cellar at the Marchbanks Estate. "I am going to enjoy this wine. Too bad I am too tired for company," said Levi. He poured a glass and took a drink of the wine; it was refreshing like Autumn told him it would be. He took a seat on the barstool and began staring off into space. From the moment Autumn boarded the plane, Kansas City was no longer home to him. He had to admit that despite his plan to befriend Autumn to get under Thomas's skin, he had grown to love her. His plan had been in the making a few years before when he met her at a nightclub downtown. She was

ROSA JAMES

underaged and trying to sneak in but security caught her red-handed. They were about to turn her away, but Levi intervened. He took responsibility for the young girl and the security let her into the club. Levi smiled before picking up his iPad from the counter and began looking up flights to Jamaica. He would go be with his friend and get a lay of the land before deciding if he would stay on a permanent basis.

After booking the flight, he closed the case on the iPad and poured another glass of wine. While savoring the fine wine, he was disturbed by a familiar voice, "You just don't guzzle Musigny." Levi turned around to see his brother, Thomas, standing in the doorway.

Levi rolled his eyes. "To what do I owe this visit? Hell, I didn't know you even knew where I lived with your bougie ass." Amused by the statement, Thomas spoke, "Oh, but you seemed to know where I laid my head, so what made you think I wouldn't find where you laid yours? You popped up at my home and disrupted my family. You knew my daughter, your niece, was being held in that bunker. And let us not forget the voicemail you left me." He walked across the kitchen to join his brother. Levi guzzled the second glass of wine down before refilling his glass, not offering any response. Entertained, Thomas continued. "Oh, you had so much to say. I heard you were the reason Autumn seduced me. So, let's talk about it, brother!"

Levi looked at him from head to toe, admiring his all-black attire. Thomas wore a Romano Lambskin Leather Jacket, Saint Laurent black jeans, a black t-shirt, and black Givenchy boots. "Looks like you road the Razor over tonight," said Levi, taking another drink of his wine. Thomas frowned. "Damn, you're drinking my wine and won't even offer me a glass. You're still such a horrible host." Levi did not budge so Thomas helped himself to a glass in the cabinet and poured the rest of the wine into his glass. Levi, who was now feeling a slight buzz, rolled his eyes. "Shit, I figured you didn't need this one measly bottle. Hell, you probably have twelve more in your wine cellar at the Marchbanks mansion!" Thomas chuckled and sipped his wine. "What is this about, Levi? You seem upset when I should be."

"Look, I went to check on Jada. It was not in the plan to hold her captive. How did you think my nephew was able to find her? Because I helped lead him to her after watching him rummage through those damn woods for months. I can't believe you are going to stand here and act like you were not the reason his mother committed suicide. Samantha was like a mother to me, and it killed me to see her hurt after you took her son and left her for that rich Marchbanks-Covington bitch. So, I set out for revenge."

Thomas took another sip of his wine. It angered him that his own brother would betray him and learning the reason why opened a door of pain that Thomas tried to keep locked away. He loved Samantha but their relationship became toxic when he started outgrowing her. Samantha was raised on love and longevity and believed that was all people needed to sustain a relationship. But Thomas had learned hard lessons with that mindset. Everyone in his environment was going nowhere except for his late brother Clayton. Being around a person for several years meant nothing to him when it came to growth. Why did he have to continue to suffer because of these stunted relationships? Thomas felt smothered and needed out that box. And with that he began losing a lot of valued relationships because of his change. It hurt the most when he started losing family. At some point, he had to move on for better days because if not, he would be still stuck. Samantha was not on board with the change.

She was content with living in the hood for the rest of her life so he had to move on.

Vita was his speed. She only made him want to be better. Despite their complicated relationships at the beginning, they never allowed any of that to sabotage their friendship. You could say they became best friends long before marriage. Having each other's back all the way. Thomas tried to honor his relationship with Samantha, but her ghetto mentality and inability to grow became unbearable. The moment Vita's husband died, Thomas knew that was his sign to move on from Samantha. He tried to break it off with her as gently as possible, but she held on to everything. She had imprinted herself within his family. Everyone thought he was wrong for not being with her because she had been there from day one. Samantha was one of the many reasons why he had strained relationships until this day with his family and Levi had been the worst. The two had a trauma bond that could not be broken. When Levi's family rejected his sexuality and lifestyle, it was Samantha that embraced him. She was the one always there before that, taking care of Levi. He would never forget the night he walked into the bathroom and found her dead in the tub.

"Levi! Never bring up Samantha to me again! I was there and I hurt just as much as you do every time I look into our son's eyes. You were young and don't understand what we went through. And no matter how you feel about anything, there was no excuse for you participating in sabotaging my family. Especially playing a role in abducting my daughter, your own niece, an innocent child! There is no coming back from this shit. That's why I am going to share a final drink with you before ending your life." Levi finished his last glass. "So this is how it ends? I see you still have that street in you! I thought the wealthy life had your ass soft like a baby's bottom."

Thomas drew his gun and aimed at Levi's chest. "You see, that's where you are wrong. I will always have street in me. I just choose to enjoy the finer things in life." Looking at the gun made Levi's stomach turn. It had been a while since he witnessed his brother put in work. Now it would be to his misfortune that he would be the next kill. Now he wished that he had taken that invite to Jamaica and left with Autumn earlier that day. Now sweating, his heart pounding. He yelled at his brother, "You know, the best thing about dying is that I will be reunited with Samantha! I will never have to think about finding her body in that tub again!"

With no response, Thomas pulled the trigger and sent two bullets into his little brother's chest. He stood over Levi and watched him take his last breath. He then washed his wine glass, took the empty wine bottle, and exited the apartment. He walked down the alley to his Razor and went home as if nothing ever happened.

Two days later, Thomas received a call from his aunt who was in a frantic. She informed him that she found Levi dead in his apartment when she went to check on him after not showing up for work. Thomas tried to be sincere and comfort his aunt. He went as far as assisting with making the funeral arrangements and paying for everything since he was the one who pulled the trigger. After attending the funeral service, Thomas instructed the funeral home to send Levi's ashes to the Marchbanks Estate. He told his aunt that Levi wanted his cremains to be spread in the Pacific Ocean and he was taking a trip to do just that. But his real plans were much more malicious.

Weeks later in Jamaica, on a bright Saturday morning in March, Autumn relaxed on her front porch. She was waiting for Kareem to finish cooking the oxtails when she received the package. She got up, walked up to the carrier, then thanked him. After observing the box with no return address, she opened it. She picked up the copper object now assuming it was a vase that Kareem ordered from the shopping network. Then she read the inscription and screamed dropping the heavy urn, almost injuring her foot. Kareem rushed outside where he found Autumn on the ground crying. Less than a foot away was the copper urn that read Levi. There was no doubt in either of their minds that Thomas was responsible for this. Kareem kneeled to her side, wrapped his arms around her and began rocking. "Don't worry, Autumn, it's only a season and we will get through this."

"The grass can be greener on both sides. It is up to you to decide what greener means to you."

MORE BOOKS BY ROSA JAMES

LOYAL SNAKES 1 & 2

HARRIS 1 & 2

MISUSE BOOK OF STORIES

ASSAD'S QUEEN

PASSION2RIGHT.COM

www.ingramcontent.com/pod-product-compliance
Lightning Source LLC
Chambersburg PA
CBHW050310260626
47156CB00005B/1734